SPIDER SANDWICHES

Claire Freedman   **Illustrated by Sue Hendra**
and Paul Linnet

BLOOMSBURY
LONDON NEW DELHI NEW YORK SYDNEY

Do come to tea with Max.
He has a MONSTER appetite!

He eats such yucky, mucky food,
his mealtimes are a fright.

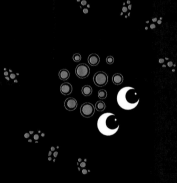

He LOVES to glug slug milkshake,
through a stinky hosepipe straw.

And as for beetle biscuits—
he can ALWAYS munch one more!

For breakfast every morning,
he chews toenail scrambled eggs.

Then guzzles down a smoothie,
made from squidged grasshopper legs!

He buys snacks on the Internet,
from as far away as space...

spiky space ants, moon-goo globs,
are all stuffed in his face!

By lunchtime Max is STARVING.
"Scrummy lice rice — I can't wait!"

He slurps it SUPER fast before
the lice crawl off his plate!

He bought the Monsters' Cookbook,
for some recipe ideas.

The best was slimed-eel noodles,
served with hairy fried bat's ears!

To pickled worms and squashed fly jam,
Max beams, "Hooray! Yes, please!"

He spreads them on his crackers —POOH—
with smelly fisheye cheese.

"So delicious!" gurgles Max,
with a massive goo-filled grin...

cold, crunchy, cockroach curry,
drip-dribbling down his chin.

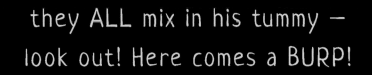

they ALL mix in his tummy —
look out! Here comes a BURP!

Rat's tail pizza, blue mould chips,
bug burgers are a treat.

But when it comes to teatime,
there's just ONE thing he will eat...

Squiggly spider sandwiches!
He shoves them in so fast.

He eats their heads and sticky webs,
but saves their legs for last!

Max will eat up anything
that oozes gunk and gloop.

But even MONSTERS gasp, "No, thanks!"
when faced with...

GREEN SPROUT SOUP!

To Michael, who's not afraid of spiders x
— CF

For lovely Steve who adores food but, unlike Max,
has impeccable table manners — SH

Bloomsbury Publishing, London, New Delhi, New York and Sydney
First published in Great Britain in 2013 by Bloomsbury Publishing Plc
50 Bedford Square, London, WC1B 3DP

Text copyright © Claire Freedman 2013
Illustrations copyright © Sue Hendra 2013
The moral rights of the author and illustrator have been asserted

A CIP catalogue record of this book is available from the British Library

ISBN 978 1 4088 3914 0 (HB)
ISBN 978 1 4088 3915 7 (PB)
ISBN 978 1 4088 3913 3 (eBook)

1 3 5 7 9 10 8 6 4 2

Printed in China by C&C Offset Printing Co Ltd, Shenzhen, Guangdong

www.bloomsbury.com

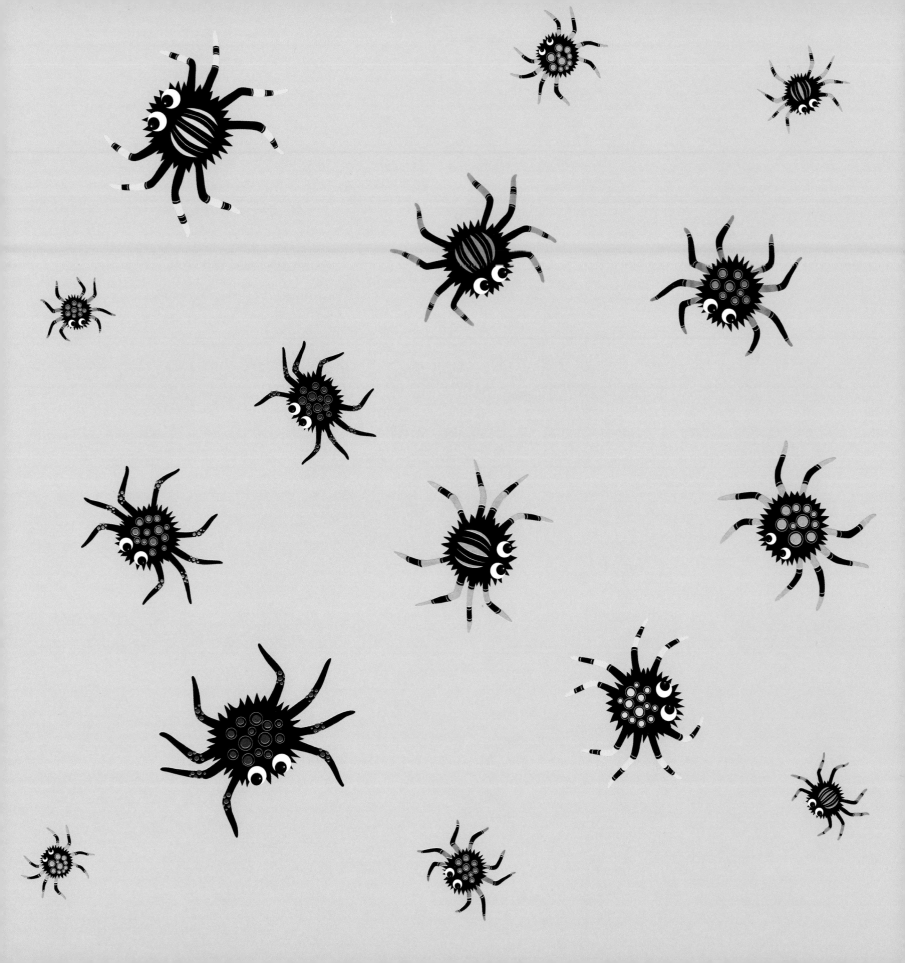